Dazzling Water Sports

Written by
Cath Jones

There are lots of water sports that we can do.

Swimming is one of the cheapest. You can see people swimming in swimming pools, in lakes, in rivers and in the sea.

Some people think that swimming in the winter is good for you.

Look at this brave mum!

Sailing is a fun water sport.

Sailing boats are light, with big sails. That way, they can go quite fast when the wind fills the sail.

These boats have an extra big sail called a **spinnaker**. This sail makes the boat go even faster.

Surfing is fantastic fun.

A surfer rides on a wave as it washes up onto the beach. So you need to surf near the coast.

Lots of surfers like to go out on big waves when the wind is strong.

This surfer is a true hot shot!

When the surfer reaches the beach, they will go back out and do it again!

Windsurfing is a mix of sailing and surfing.

You are surfing, but you do not need waves to keep going. You grab a sail and the wind drives you on.

Windsurfers can go fast.

Some windsurfers even flip upside-down!

This is kite surfing. People call it an extreme sport, as you can go **so** fast!

It is a bit like windsurfing, but you have a kite, not a sail. The kite harnesses the power of the wind.

Good kite surfers can leap high into the air.

Do you want to have a go?

Do not let go!

Foil surfing is quite a new sport.

This is a foil. It looks like a fin with wings. The foil is beneath the platform that you stand on.

The foil makes the platform rise up into the air.

You can speed across the water on one of these!

Dragon boating is a team sport.

The crew sit in pairs in the dragon boat. They are the **paddlers**. They make the boat go.

Each boat has a drummer to help the paddlers keep time. Can you see the drummer? Where is he?

Each boat has a **steerer** too. He steers the boat!

Who do you think will win?

After the water sports are finished, it's time for something to eat.

Do you think they will have some bagels with butter and jam?

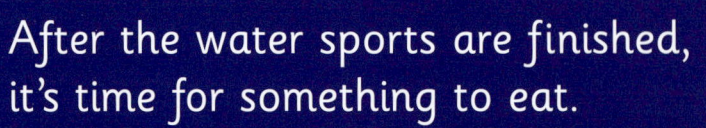